To Christopher, Alexandra, Jonathan, Steven,
Michael, Albert, Frances, Sam, and Cecile
—B.I. and S.W.

Clarion Books
Ticknor & Fields, a Houghton Mifflin Company
Copyright © 1982 by North American Bear Co., Inc.
Printed in the United States of America

Library of Congress Cataloging in Publication Data

Isenberg, Barbara. The adventures of Albert, the running bear.
Summary: Following his escape from the zoo, Albert Bear en-
counters a series of mishaps and finally finds himself running in
a marathon.
[1. Runaways—Fiction. 2. Running—Fiction. 3. Bears—Fiction]
I. Gackenbach, Dick, ill. II. Title.
PZ7.I774Al   [E]   82-1311   ISBN 0-89919-113-4   AACR2
Paperback ISBN 0-89919-125-8

Y 10 9 8 7

THE ADVENTURES OF ALBERT, THE RUNNING BEAR

by Barbara Isenberg and Susan Wolf

Illustrated by Dick Gackenbach

CLARION BOOKS

TICKNOR AND FIELDS: A HOUGHTON MIFFLIN COMPANY

NEW YORK

Albert was a trained circus bear. But when his circus went out of business, he was moved to a zoo. The zoo was in the middle of a green park, in the middle of a big, busy city.

Albert's cage was large and clean. He had friendly neighbors on either side, nice toys, four meals a day, and a kind keeper named Norman. Although Albert was happy, he still missed the circus. Most of all, he missed making people laugh and cheer.

One day, Albert decided to practice the waltz he used to do in the circus. As he pranced and twirled, a crowd began to gather.

When Albert saw people smiling, he broke into a silly, wobbly kind of dance. The crowd began to laugh.

Next he grabbed his dinner bowl, turned it upside down on his head, wiggled his hips, and did the hula. The crowd cheered.

Then Albert picked up the three fish that had fallen out of his bowl and juggled them in the air. The crowd went wild with applause.

Albert took his final bow, but the crowd began to chant, "We want more. WE WANT MORE." So Albert did his tricks again.

Soon Albert was performing to huge crowds every day. He loved hearing the applause and laughter again. But even more, he loved the food the crowds threw to him. The sign on his cage said, PLEASE DO NOT FEED THIS ANIMAL, but people were always rewarding him with delicious snacks.

Albert could not get enough of those tasty treats. There were fluffy bits of cotton candy, pointy ends of ice cream cones, chocolate bars, bubble gum, and buttery popcorn. Albert's two favorites were marshmallows and gumdrops.

PLEASE DO NOT
FEED
THIS ANIMAL

One day, Norman brought the zoo doctor in to examine Albert.
"Just look at that flab," the doctor said as he poked his finger into
Albert's big fat belly.

"You must stop eating all those snacks and stick to the healthy
meals we feed you here," the doctor warned.

But Albert didn't stop eating those snacks. In fact, he soon stopped eating the zoo meals and ate ONLY snacks.

"Mmm, mmm, this is the life!" Albert thought as he held out his dinner bowl like a catcher's mitt while the crowd filled it with his favorites. Then he opened his mouth and slurped down the whole bowlful in one gulp.

The sign in the image reads: THIS BEAR MUST NOT BE FED SNACKS. ANYONE CAUGHT FEEDING HIM WILL BE FINED $100.00

One day, a new sign appeared on Albert's cage. It said: THIS BEAR MUST NOT BE FED SNACKS. ANYONE CAUGHT FEEDING HIM WILL BE FINED $100.00. No one threw Albert anything that day. Or the next. Or the next.

By the night of the fourth day, Albert was feeling very low. He lay in a fat heap on the bottom of his cage, muttering, "Marshmallows and gumdrops, marshmallows and gumdrops."

"Maybe I could reach a little something for you," offered Julia the giraffe, who was Albert's neighbor. She knew she shouldn't help Albert go off his diet, but she hated to see her friend so sad.

"I have an idea!" cried Albert suddenly.

"What is it?" asked Julia.

"Bend your head down into my cage," said Albert, "and I'll show you."

Julia thought Albert was going to whisper his plan into her ear. Instead, he wrapped his arms tightly around her neck and shouted, "Lift, Julia! Lift me to the wall!"

Julia was so surprised that she did what Albert ordered. Her neck rose like a great crane, with Albert dangling on the end. She placed him on top of the wall dividing their cages, and Albert tight-rope walked across the narrow wall to the bars.

"Thank you, Julia," Albert whispered as he slid down the bars to freedom. "Gumdrops and marshmallows, here I come!"

When Albert could no longer see the zoo behind him, he stopped to catch his breath. "Where can I get myself a little snack?" he wondered. Just then the moon disappeared behind the clouds and it began to pour.

Albert ran for shelter, stumbled into a trash can, and knocked it over. "This place will be dry," he thought, as he crawled inside. He wiggled and squirmed, trying to get comfortable. Then his nose began to twitch. He smelled food.

Albert smacked around the small space with his great big paw until he hit something soft and gooey. Mmm, mmm. It was a piece of an ice cream sandwich. He stuffed it in his mouth. Next, he found half a box of Cracker Jack, a can of fizzy cola, a crunchy candy bar, some potato chips, pickles, pretzels, and a hot dog bun.

"What a wonderful place this is!" hiccupped Albert, as he drifted off to sleep.

CRASH, SMASH. A terrible jolt awakened Albert. His trash can had just been dumped into the loading bin of a garbage truck. He sat up and rubbed his big belly. "Ohhh, do I feel awful! I wish I were back in my nice cozy cage."

Albert rocked back and forth, moaning and groaning. A blue cloth bag caught his eye. He grabbed the bag and stuck his paw inside.

"This feels nice," thought Albert, as he pulled out a beautiful, red sweatshirt. He put it on, pulled up the hood, and tied the drawstring.

He reached in the bag again. This time he took out a pair of sweat pants, which he stepped into, and a pair of sneakers, which he put on.

I inform he is going to be in a race.

d the
ns of
di-
lbert

didn't know it, but the Annual City Marathon had just begun.

Albert watched them go by and wondered what they were running from.

Suddenly, the sanitation man turned on the garbage compactor. WHRRRR! MUNCH! CRUNCH!

"Yikes!" yelled Albert. "Whatever it is, it's coming after me!" He leaped off the truck in terror. Down the park path he zoomed, past a man with the number 24 pinned to his shirt.

"Hey, young fellow!" said Number 24 to Albert, not realizing Albert was a bear. "You'd better take it easy. You'll never be able to keep up that pace!"

So Albert slowed down. And, since the man seemed helpful and nice, Albert followed him out of the park and onto the crowded city streets.

As Number 24 turned the corner of the Marathon course, Albert lost sight of him. He was confused by the honking horns and pushing people. How he longed to get back to the quiet and safety of his cage. Never would he go looking for snacks again!

A blue bus roared by. On the back, Albert spotted a picture of his own zoo.

"I'll follow that bus home," Albert thought. He ran along behind, coughing from the fumes. The bus picked up speed, and Albert couldn't run any faster. He stopped to rest. His muscles ached, his fur was dripping with sweat, and his mouth was as dry as cotton wool.

But even worse, he was lost. Utterly lost. He sat down on a curb, put his head between his paws, and began to cry.

Then Albert heard a familiar voice. "Don't give up now, old
buddy," the voice said. "Let's go!"

It was Number 24 again. He pulled Albert up by the sleeve into
the middle of a pack of running people.

Albert was moving at just the right pace. He was beginning to enjoy the feeling of running, and did not notice when Number 24 let go of his sleeve and dropped behind.

Albert passed one group of runners. And then another group. He had hit his stride!

Albert's arms and legs and heart and breath were all working together. He felt better than he had ever felt in his life. He did not realize he had come back into the park, or see the crowd that had come to watch the end of the Marathon. Nor did he see the white tape that stretched across his path only a few yards away. Albert was moving as if he were in a dream.

Suddenly . . .

"SNAP!" went the tape.

"FLASH!" popped the camera bulbs.

"HOORAY!" cheered the crowd.

"Uh-oh," gulped Albert, as he saw the crowd rushing toward him. He spotted a platform and ran for cover.

An arm reached under and pulled Albert out and up onto the platform. The arm belonged to the Mayor, who was smiling. Albert grinned back nervously.

"Congratulations, young man!" the Mayor said, not realizing Albert was a bear. "You have just won the Annual Marathon Race," he continued. And he handed Albert a beautiful, gleaming trophy. The crowd cheered again, and the band began to play.

At the sound of the music, Albert started to dance. He wiggled and swayed and twisted and twirled. The more the crowd cheered, the more Albert danced.

At last the Mayor signaled the band to stop playing. The newspaper photographers asked Albert and the Mayor to pose together.

"Wait a minute!" said the Mayor, as he reached up and pulled back Albert's hood for the photo. The Mayor's mouth dropped into a perfect "O". "You're a bear!" he gasped. There was a long silence.

"Why, Albert, old rascal! It's you!" someone called out from the crowd. It was Norman, the zoo keeper.

Then the crowd buzzed. "It's Albert! It's Albert, the performing bear from the zoo!"

"It's Albert, the Running Bear, now!" the Mayor said. Albert ran a few steps in place and waved his trophy. Everyone laughed and got in line for his paw-print. Keeper Norman was the last person in line.

"You're a celebrity now, Albert," Norman said. "Do you still want to come back to the zoo?"

Without a moment's hesitation, Albert jumped into the zoo van.

When they got back to the zoo, Norman promised to build a quarter-mile track for Albert to keep in shape. Albert promised he would never run away again and never eat snacks. Well...maybe just a few marshmallows and gumdrops now and then.

Every morning now, Albert gets up, puts on his sweat suit, and runs on the track.

And the crowds are bigger than ever.